little Miss Neat

by Roger Hargreaves

Little Miss Neat was a very tidy person.

Probably the tidiest person in the world.

She lived in Twopin Cottage.

It was called Twopin Cottage because she kept it as neat as two pins!

She just couldn't stand a mess.

Every day she spent all day polishing and dusting and cleaning and making sure that things were in their proper places.

One morning little Miss Neat awoke in her bedroom at Twopin Cottage.

She looked out of her bedroom window.

It had been raining during the night, and there was a puddle in the middle of her garden path.

"Oh," she gasped in horror, and rushed outside with a duster.

She mopped up every drop of puddle, and then she rushed inside and washed the duster, and then she ironed the duster, and then she folded the duster, and then she placed the duster very neatly back in its drawer.

Everything in Twopin Cottage had its proper place!

Now, this story is about the time little Miss Neat went on holiday.

She always went away for one week every summer, and this year was no different.

She spent two weeks packing.

And then she spent a whole day polishing her suitcase.

And then off she set leaving Twopin Cottage all spick and span and neat and tidy.

"Oh I hope it doesn't get too dusty while I'm away," she thought as she closed the door behind her.

But something worse than dusty was going to happen to Twopin Cottage.

Would you like to know what?

Mr Muddle came to tea!

He'd written to Miss Neat to tell her, but, being Mr Muddle, he somehow got into a muddle posting the letter.

Actually, what happened was that when Mr Muddle went to post the letter he had the letter in one hand and a half-eaten sandwich in the other.

And you can guess what happened, can't you?

That's right!

He posted the sandwich!

A posted cheese sandwich!

"It'll be nice seeing Miss Neat again,"
he chuckled to himself as he walked home.

"This sandwich is a bit chewy," he thought.

It was the day after Miss Neat left that
Mr Muddle arrived.

He walked up the garden path of Twopin
Cottage, and knocked at the door.

No reply!

"Goodbye!" he shouted.

It should have been "Hello!" but he isn't
called Mr Muddle for nothing.

"Nobody home?" he called.

He pushed open the door.

"Oh dear," he thought as he looked around.

"Nobody home!"

"Never mind," he thought. "I'll make myself a cup of tea and wait for Miss Neat."

So he went into the kitchen of Twopin Cottage, made himself a cup of tea, and waited.

And waited.

And waited.

And waited.

And went home.

Little Miss Neat stepped out of the taxi outside Twopin Cottage.

"That was a lovely holiday," she said, paying the taxi driver. "But it's nice to be home."

She walked up the garden path, and went in through the door.

"Not too dusty," she said to herself looking around.

"I think I'll make myself a nice cup of tea before I start unpacking."

But, making tea after a Mr Muddle visit isn't quite as easy as it sounds.

Little Miss Neat eventually found the teapot.

Not in its proper place.

In the refrigerator!

And she eventually found the milk.

Not in its proper place.

In the teapot!

And the tea.

In the sugar bowl!

And the sugar.

In the milk jug!

And a cup.

In the oven!

And a saucer.

In the breadbin!

But, could she find a teaspoon?

She could not!

The telephone rang.

Little Miss Neat picked it up.

"Hello," she said.

At the other end of the line Mr Muddle suddenly realised he was holding the telephone the wrong way round.

He turned it the right way round.

"Goodbye," he said.

"Who's that?" asked Miss Neat.

"It's you," replied Mr Muddle.

Miss Neat thought.

"It's Mr Muddle, isn't it?" she guessed.

"Yes," replied Mr Muddle, getting it right for once.

"And you paid me a visit while I was away on holiday, didn't you?" she guessed again.

"Yes," replied Mr Muddle, getting it right for twice.

"Can I come and see you now you're back?"

"I suppose so," sighed Miss Neat.

"Goodbye!"

"Hello!" said Mr Muddle.

And put the 'phone down.

Little Miss Neat sighed a heavy sigh, and sat down in the armchair next to the telephone.

Ouch!!

She looked underneath the cushion.

There were all her teaspoons.

And knives!

And forks!

I don't think little Miss Neat will be taking a holiday next year.

Do you?

3 Great Offers for MR. MEN Fans!

MR.MEN TOKEN

1 New Mr. Men or Little Miss Library Bus Presentation Cases

A brand new stronger, roomier school bus library box, with sturdy carrying handle and stay-closed fasteners.

The full colour, wipe-clean boxes make a great home for your full collection.

They're just £5.99 inc P&P and free bookmark!

☐ MR. MEN ☐ LITTLE MISS (please tick and order overleaf)

2 Door Hangers and Posters

In every Mr. Men and Little Miss book like this one, you will find a special token. Collect 6 tokens and we will send you a brilliant Mr. Men or Little Miss poster and a Mr. Men or Little Miss double sided full colour bedroom door hanger of your choice. Simply tick your choice in the list and tape a 50p coin for your two items to this page.

PLEASE STICK YOUR 50P COIN HERE

Door Hangers (please tick)
☐ Mr. Nosey & Mr. Muddle
☐ Mr. Slow & Mr. Busy
☐ Mr. Messy & Mr. Quiet
☐ Mr. Perfect & Mr. Forgetful
☐ Little Miss Fun & Little Miss Late
☐ Little Miss Helpful & Little Miss Tidy
☐ Little Miss Busy & Little Miss Brainy
☐ Little Miss Star & Little Miss Fun

Posters (please tick)
☐ MR.MEN
☐ LITTLE MISS

3 Sixteen Beautiful Fridge Magnets – any 2 for £2.00! inc.P&P

They're very special collector's items!
Simply tick your first and second* choices from the list below
of any 2 characters!

1st Choice

☐ Mr. Happy
☐ Mr. Lazy
☐ Mr. Topsy-Turvy
☐ Mr. Bounce
☐ Mr. Bump
☐ Mr. Small
☐ Mr. Snow
☐ Mr. Wrong

☐ Mr. Daydream
☐ Mr. Tickle
☐ Mr. Greedy
☐ Mr. Funny
☐ Little Miss Giggles
☐ Little Miss Splendid
☐ Little Miss Naughty
☐ Little Miss Sunshine

2nd Choice

☐ Mr. Happy
☐ Mr. Lazy
☐ Mr. Topsy-Turvy
☐ Mr. Bounce
☐ Mr. Bump
☐ Mr. Small
☐ Mr. Snow
☐ Mr. Wrong

☐ Mr. Daydream
☐ Mr. Tickle
☐ Mr. Greedy
☐ Mr. Funny
☐ Little Miss Giggles
☐ Little Miss Splendid
☐ Little Miss Naughty
☐ Little Miss Sunshine

*Only in case your first choice is out of stock.

--- TO BE COMPLETED BY AN ADULT ---

**To apply for any of these great offers, ask an adult to complete the coupon below and send it with
the appropriate payment and tokens, if needed, to MR. MEN OFFERS, PO BOX 7, MANCHESTER M19 2HD**

☐ Please send ____ Mr. Men Library case(s) and/or ____ Little Miss Library case(s) at £5.99 each inc P&P

☐ Please send a poster and door hanger as selected overleaf. I enclose six tokens plus a 50p coin for P&P

☐ Please send me ____ pair(s) of Mr. Men/Little Miss fridge magnets, as selected above at £2.00 inc P&P

Fan's Name _____

Address _____

_____ **Postcode** _____

Date of Birth _____

Name of Parent/Guardian _____

Total amount enclosed £ _____

☐ **I enclose a cheque/postal order payable to Egmont Books Limited**

☐ **Please charge my MasterCard/Visa/Amex/Switch or Delta account** (delete as appropriate)

Card Number

Expiry date ___/___   **Signature** _____

Please allow 28 days for delivery. We reserve the right to change the terms of this offer at any time
but we offer a 14 day money back guarantee. This does not affect your statutory rights.

MR.MEN   LITTLE MISS
Mr. Men and Little Miss™ & ©Mrs. Roger Hargreaves

CUT ALONG DOTTED LINE AND RETURN THIS WHOLE PAGE